"You were alone in her house?"

Marvin nodded.

"Oh, man, what'd you do?" asked Nick.

Marvin shrugged.

"Let me see the key," said Stuart.

Marvin fished the key out of his pocket.

Stuart took it from him. "Wow," he said, then handed it to Nick.

"Hey, everybody!" Nick shouted. "I have the key to Mrs. North's house!"

First Stepping Stone Books you will enjoy:

By David A. Adler
(The Houdini Club Magic Mystery series)
Onion Sundaes

By Mary Pope Osborne
(The Magic Tree House series)
Dinosaurs Before Dark (#1)
The Knight at Dawn (#2)
Mummies in the Morning (#3)
Pirates Past Noon (#4)

By Barbara Park
Junie B. Jones and the Stupid Smelly Bus
Junie B. Jones and a Little Monkey Business
Junie B. Jones and Her Big Fat Mouth
Junie B. Jones and Some Sneaky Peeky Spying

By Louis Sachar
Marvin Redpost: Kidnapped at Birth?
Marvin Redpost: Why Pick on Me?
Marvin Redpost: Is He a Girl?
Marvin Redpost: Alone in His Teacher's House

By Marjorie Weinman Sharmat
The Great Genghis Khan Look-Alike Contest
Genghis Khan: A Dog Star Is Born

MARVIN REDPOST:
Alone in His Teacher's House

by Louis Sachar

illustrated by Barbara Sullivan

A FIRST STEPPING STONE BOOK

Random House 🏠 New York

Dedicated to François, Xavier, Myriam,
and Bruno.
In memory of Cartouche.

Text copyright © 1994 by Louis Sachar
Illustrations copyright © 1994 by Barbara Sullivan
Cover illustration copyright © 1994 by Neal Hughes
All rights reserved under International and Pan-American
Copyright Conventions. Published in the United States by
Random House, Inc., New York, and simultaneously in Canada
by Random House of Canada Limited, Toronto.

Library of Congress Cataloging-in-Publication Data
Sachar, Louis. Marvin Redpost : alone in his teacher's
house / by Louis Sachar ; illustrated by Barbara Sullivan.
p. cm. "A First stepping stone book."
SUMMARY: Marvin is pleased when his teacher asks him to take
care of her dog while she's away, but he soon finds that there's
more pressure involved than he likes.
ISBN 0-679-81949-5 (trade) — ISBN 0-679-91949-X (lib. bdg.)
[1. Dogs—Fiction. 2. Pets—Fiction. 3. Teachers—Fiction.
4. Responsibility—Fiction.]
I. Sullivan, Barbara, ill. II. Title.
PZ7.S1185Man 1994 [Fic]—dc20 93-19791
Manufactured in the United States of America
10 9 8 7 6 5 4 3 2 1

Random House, Inc. New York, Toronto, London, Sydney, Auckland

Contents

1
Teacher's Pet

"You will have a substitute teacher tomorrow," Mrs. North told her third-grade class.

"All right!" shouted Nick.

Mrs. North stared at Nick.

Marvin Redpost looked down at his desk and smiled. Nick Tuffle was Marvin's best friend. Marvin had two best friends. His other best friend was Stuart Albright.

"I will be gone for one week," said Mrs. North. "I won't be back until next Thursday. A week from tomorrow."

"Hot dog!" exclaimed Nick.

Mrs. North glared at Nick. "I will leave detailed instructions for the substitute," she warned. "And if any of you misbehave, I will know about it. That means you, Nick."

"Hey, why pick on me?" asked Nick.

When it was time to go home, Nick and Stuart gathered around Marvin's desk.

"A substitute for a week!" said Nick, rubbing his hands together. "This is going to be great."

"Let's pretend we're each other," said Stuart. "I'll be Marvin. Marvin, you be Nick. And Nick, you can be me."

"I don't want to be *you*," Nick said to Stuart. "I'll be Marvin, and you be me."

"I don't want to be *you!*" said Stuart.

It made Marvin feel proud that both

his friends wanted to be him.

On the other hand, he wasn't sure he wanted either of them to be him.

"Marvin, may I talk to you for a moment?" asked Mrs. North.

"What'd you do?" asked Stuart.

Marvin shrugged. He didn't think he did anything.

And even if he did, what could Mrs. North do about it? She was going away for a week.

He walked to her desk.

"Do you like dogs?" asked Mrs. North.

"Sure," he said.

"I'm going to need someone to take care of Waldo while I'm away," said Mrs. North.

"Waldo?" asked Marvin.

"I was going to put him in a kennel,"

said Mrs. North. "But he's such an old dog. It would be so much nicer if he could stay home."

Marvin could hardly believe his ears.

"I'll pay you three dollars a day," said Mrs. North. "Times seven days. That's twenty-one dollars. Tell you what. I'll give you a four dollar bonus if there are no problems. Twenty-five dollars."

Marvin nodded his head. He was too shocked to speak.

"Good," said Mrs. North. "You want to come to my house now and meet Waldo?"

Marvin stared at her. "Okay," he said.

"I'll call your mother," said Mrs. North. "And I've got a few things to finish up. I'll meet you in the parking lot in twenty minutes."

"Okay."

Stuart and Nick were waiting outside for him.

"Did you get in trouble?" asked Nick.

"No," said Marvin, still in shock.

"You want to play soccer?" asked Stuart.

"I can't," said Marvin. "I have to meet Mrs. North in the parking lot. She's going to drive me in her car."

"Her car!" said Nick.

"To her house," said Marvin.

"Her house!" said Stuart.

"She's going to pay me to take care of her dog while she's away."

His friends stared at him wide-eyed.

"Three dollars a day. Plus a bonus of four dollars if there are no problems."

"Twenty-five bucks," said Stuart. He was good at math.

"You are *so* lucky," said Nick. "You're the luckiest kid in the whole world."

2
The Key

Marvin's friends waited with him in the parking lot.

"Which one do you think is her car?" asked Stuart.

"I don't know," said Marvin.

"I can't believe you guys are so dumb!" said Nick. "She drives that yellow Firebird. Over there, next to Mrs. Grant's red Cougar. The pick-up truck is Mr. McCabe's. The van is Mr. Gurdy's. I can tell you every teacher's car."

"But you've never driven in one," said Stuart, patting Marvin on the back.

Mrs. North came out of the office. She held a folder filled with papers.

"Are you ready, Marvin?" she asked.

He nodded.

"We just wanted to watch him get into your car," said Stuart.

Mrs. North smiled. "Well, it's that yellow one, over there."

"*I know,*" said Nick.

Mrs. North and Marvin walked across the parking lot.

"May I carry that for you?" Marvin asked.

"Thank you, Marvin," said Mrs. North. She handed him the folder. "It's my homework," she told him.

"*You* have homework?"

"Sure. I have to correct *your* homework. In fact, I have a lot more homework than you. I have to correct your homework, plus the homework of every student in the class."

"Hmm," said Marvin. He never thought of that before.

She unlocked the door of her car, got in, then reached over and unlocked Marvin's door.

He sat down next to her.

"You have a very nice car," he said.

"Thank you," said Mrs. North.

"The seat is very comfortable."

"I'm glad you like it," said Mrs. North.

He tugged gently on the seat belt. "The seat belt seems nice and strong," he said.

"Good," said Mrs. North. "In case I crash."

She started the engine. They drove off.

Marvin waved out the window to his two best friends. Then he leaned back and enjoyed the ride.

From the outside, Mrs. North's house just looked like a normal house. Marvin didn't know what he expected. Maybe a flagpole in front? He wondered if her neighbors even knew she was a teacher.

They parked in the garage and walked inside through the laundry room.

Waldo was waiting for them. His long black tail swished slowly behind him.

He was a big dog with graying black hair. His face was covered with long gray whiskers, almost white.

He looked like a walrus.

"Waldo, I'd like you to meet Marvin,"

Mrs. North said very politely. "Marvin, this is Waldo."

"Nice to meet you, Waldo," Marvin said.

"He's seventeen years old," said Mrs. North. "That's a hundred and nineteen in dog years."

Marvin petted the old dog and scratched him behind the ears.

Mrs. North showed Marvin around her house. Waldo followed. He waddled like a walrus when he walked.

"You just live in a regular house," said Marvin.

Mrs. North laughed. "What did you expect? A blackboard in the living room?"

He laughed.

Waldo made a whining noise. It was almost like he was singing.

Mrs. North bent down and petted him. "Oh, Wa-wa-wa-Waldo," she said, her nose almost touching his. "I'm going to miss you, Wa-wa-wa-Waldo!"

Waldo licked her right on the mouth.

Marvin couldn't believe it. Mrs. North was almost like a real person.

"Would you like something to eat?" she asked. "I've got chocolate chip cookies."

"No, thank you."

"I'll be gone a week. They'll go stale if nobody eats them."

"Okay," said Marvin.

While Marvin had cookies and milk, Mrs. North showed him where she kept Waldo's bowls, the leash, and the bag of dog food.

He had to fill the bowls whenever they got low. And he had to walk Waldo three times a day. Before school, after school, and in the evening.

"Oh, and here's his pooper-scooper," said Mrs. North. "You know what this is for?"

Marvin nodded as he swallowed a cookie.

She wrote down the phone number of Waldo's vet, just in case.

She also asked Marvin to bring in her mail and newspapers.

"So, any questions?"

Marvin only had one question. "Why'd you pick me?"

Mrs. North smiled. "You don't think I'd let Nick alone in my house, do you?"

Marvin smiled.

"I don't know," Mrs. North said, more seriously. "I feel I can trust you, Marvin. I think you are mature and responsible."

Marvin suddenly felt very mature and responsible.

"Oh, I almost forgot," she said. "The key."

She gave Marvin the key to her house.

3

Mature and Responsible

Marvin woke up early, got dressed, brushed his teeth, and made his bed. *He had a job to do.*

The key was in his pocket.

He was already downstairs, eating breakfast, when his mother knocked on his bedroom door and said, "Marvin, time to get up."

His father smiled at him across the kitchen table. "I'm very proud of you, Marvin," he said. "You seem to be taking your job very seriously."

Marvin nodded. But he knew it was not yet time to feel proud. Wait seven days. If he didn't lose the key. If Mrs. North's house didn't burn down. If Waldo wasn't dead. Then he'd be proud.

He finished eating, rinsed his dishes, and put them in the dishwasher.

"Oh, here you are," said his mother, coming into the kitchen. "What would you like for breakfast?"

The whole family stood by the door as Marvin left for work. Marvin had one brother and one sister. Jacob was eleven. Linzy was four.

"Twenty-five bucks! All right, Mar!" said Jacob.

Marvin slapped his big brother's hand.

It was odd. Marvin had always looked

up to Jacob. He wanted to be just like him.

But Jacob never had a job.

"I'm going to miss you, Marvin," said Linzy.

"I'm not moving away," Marvin told her. "I'll be home after school, just like every other day."

"I'll still miss you," said Linzy. "I miss you every day."

"I'll miss you too," said Marvin. He walked out the door.

There was a fence around the Redpost house. The fence was all white except for one red post.

Marvin tapped the family post—for luck—then rode his bike to Mrs. North's.

He could hear Waldo whining—or

singing—as he took the key out of his pocket.

"Hi, Waldo," he said through the door.

He unlocked the door, then carefully opened it so the dog couldn't run out.

Waldo was sitting on the other side of the door. His big tail swept back and forth.

"How ya doin', Whisker-face?" said Marvin. He petted the old dog.

Waldo didn't want Marvin to stop petting him. Every time Marvin stopped, Waldo whined and nuzzled Marvin for more.

"Oh, Waldo," said Marvin. He rubbed Waldo's head and scratched him behind the ears. "You want to go for a walk?"

He got Waldo's leash and the pooper-scooper.

They walked around the block.

It was only a little gross using the pooper-scooper. Marvin didn't let it bother him. It was his job. He was mature and responsible.

When they got back, he checked Waldo's bowls. Waldo still had plenty of food and water.

Before leaving, Marvin made sure the key was in his pocket.

Waldo whined.

Marvin petted him. "I've got to go now, Waldo," he said.

Waldo nuzzled him.

Marvin petted him some more. "I'll be back right after school," he promised.

Waldo lifted his big paw and put it on Marvin's arm.

"Okay, just a little longer," said Marvin.

Waldo rolled over and Marvin rubbed
his tummy.

4

The Substitute

"You were alone in her house?" Stuart exclaimed.

Marvin nodded.

"Oh, man, what'd you do?" asked Nick.

Marvin shrugged.

They were out on the playground. School hadn't started yet.

"Let me see the key," said Stuart.

"Did you look in her closet?" asked Nick.

"No," said Marvin. *Why would he look in her closet?*

"How about her refrigerator?" asked

Nick. "Did you at least look in her refrigerator?"

"Let me see the key," Stuart said again.

"How about her bathroom?" asked Nick.

"I don't remember," said Marvin.

"You don't remember if you saw her bathroom?" asked Nick.

"Let me see the key," said Stuart.

Marvin fished the key out of his pocket.

Stuart took it from him. "Wow," he said, then handed it to Nick.

"Hey, everybody!" Nick shouted. "I have the key to Mrs. North's house!"

Kids came running from all directions.

"Marvin was alone in her house!" said Nick as he gave the key to Kenny.

"Did you look in her closet?" asked Clarence.

"What for?" asked Marvin.

"To see her clothes!" Nick and Clarence answered together.

"Did you turn on her television?" asked Melanie.

Marvin couldn't tell who had the key anymore. It was being passed around.

"Did you use her bathroom?" asked Casey.

"He doesn't even remember if he *saw* her bathroom!" said Nick.

"What if you were alone in her house?" asked Casey. "And you had to go to the bathroom. Real bad. What would you do?"

"I'd use her bathroom," said Marvin.

Everybody laughed.

"She didn't say I couldn't," said Marvin.

They laughed harder.

The bell rang.

Everyone started to class.

"Wait!" called Marvin. "Where's—"

"Here, Marvin," said Patsy Gatsby, behind him.

She gave him the key.

As he walked into class, he heard Melanie announce, "Marvin's going to use the bathroom in Mrs. North's house!"

Several kids laughed.

"Who's Marvin?" asked the substitute teacher, standing at the front of the room.

Melanie and Warren pointed at Marvin as he made his way to his desk. He sat down.

The teacher stared at Marvin a long time. "I don't appreciate that kind of talk, Marvin," she said.

Marvin didn't know why she was picking on him. It was Melanie who said it.

Her name was Miss Hillway. She wrote it on the board.

"I'll be your teacher for a week," she said. "So let's all try to get off to a good start. That includes you, Marvin."

Patsy Gatsby sneezed.

"Bless you," said Miss Hillway.

"Thank you," Patsy said shyly, wiping her nose on her sleeve.

Nick leaned back in his chair, took a great big breath, then sneezed as loud as he could.

Miss Hillway smiled at Nick. "Bless you," she said.

Casey Happleton sat next to Marvin.

She had a ponytail that stuck out of the side of her head. Not the back.

Casey held her nose and said, "Ah-ah-ah-CHooooooooooo!" Her sideways ponytail bounced up and down.

Miss Hillway didn't bless her.

Stuart sneezed. Travis sneezed.

"Sneeze, Marvin," whispered Casey.

"Why?"

"It's funny," said Casey.

"No, it isn't," said Marvin. It was silly. *No wonder Mrs. North asked me to take care of Waldo,* he thought.

"You think you're so great," whispered Casey. "Just because you went to the bathroom in Mrs. North's house!"

Gina sneezed. Heather sneezed.

"My, there must be a terrible cold going around," said Miss Hillway.

Everyone—except Marvin—laughed.

Kenny sneezed.

Then, Miss Hillway sneezed!

A whole bunch of kids blessed her.

"Okay, that's enough," Miss Hillway said. "I hope we all got our sneezes out. Now, let's get back to work."

Clarence sneezed.

Miss Hillway didn't smile. "I'm serious now. I don't want to hear another sneeze," she warned.

"But what if you really have to?" asked Melanie.

"You can't punish someone for sneezing," said Nick.

"It's dangerous to hold back a sneeze," said Stuart. "My dad's a doctor. He knows."

"It could explode out your ears," said Casey. "You could die!"

Miss Hillway raised her eyebrows.

Marvin felt a tickle in his nose.

It was a small tickle at first. But it slowly grew, bigger and bigger inside his little nose.

He tried to hold it back, but it felt like it would explode out his ears.

He sneezed.

Miss Hillway stared at him as she slowly shook her head. "You never know when to quit, do you, Marvin?"

5

Nothing In—Nothing Out

It did not get any better for Marvin. No matter what he said or did, Miss Hillway took it the wrong way. On Friday, she called him a "hooligan."

"I don't even know what a hooligan is," Marvin said after school.

"Don't worry about it," said Stuart. "Mrs. North won't get mad at you. You're taking care of her dog."

"You can do *anything!*" said Nick. "You're so lucky. You're the luckiest kid in the whole world!"

Marvin shrugged.

That was another problem. He wasn't doing such a good job of taking care of Mrs. North's dog. Waldo hadn't eaten anything since Mrs. North left. His bowl was still full of the same old dog food.

He unlocked his bicycle.

"Can I come with you to Mrs. North's house?" asked Stuart.

Marvin looked at Stuart. Then at Nick.

Mrs. North didn't exactly *say* he couldn't bring his friends over.

"Sorry," he said.

"Why not?" asked Stuart. "I'm not going to wreck anything."

Marvin wasn't worried about Stuart. But if he said yes to Stuart, then Nick would want to come too.

"Mrs. North said she doesn't want anyone else in her house," he lied.

"I just want to sit in her chair," said Nick.

"She won't find out," said Stuart.

"I just want to turn her lights on and off," said Nick.

"Sorry," said Marvin. "It's her rule. Not mine." He got on his bike. "I'll see you later, okay?"

His friends stared at him.

He rode off. He felt bad lying to his two best friends. But he just didn't want to take any chances.

He glanced back. Nick and Stuart were on their bikes, a half a block behind him.

He turned a corner and stopped.

Nick and Stuart came around the corner, then stopped when they saw him.

"You can't come to her house!" said Marvin.

"We're just riding our bikes," Stuart said.

"Mrs. North doesn't own the streets," said Nick.

"Well, quit following me."

"We're not following you!" said Nick. "He thinks we're following him."

"Just a coincidence," Stuart explained.

Marvin got back on his bike. Stuart and Nick followed.

He stopped in front of Mrs. North's house. Stuart and Nick stopped too.

"Just taking a rest," said Stuart. He stretched his arms and yawned.

Marvin went into his teacher's house and locked the door behind him.

Waldo's bowl was still full.

"Oh, Wa-wa-wa-Waldo," said Marvin, petting him.

Waldo's tail swept the floor.

"You really have to eat," he told the old dog.

Waldo whined and nuzzled Marvin.

Marvin petted him. "Nick and Stuart are so immature," he said. "You're lucky I'm taking care of you, and not them."

He hooked on the leash, grabbed the pooper-scooper, and led Waldo outside.

"That's the ugliest dog I've ever seen," laughed Nick.

"It looks like a walrus!" said Stuart.

"C'mon, Waldo," said Marvin.

"Waldo?" Nick and Stuart said together.

"Where's Waldo?" said Nick.

They laughed again.

Marvin tugged on the leash, but Waldo didn't seem to want to take a walk. He just took two steps and sat down. He looked back at the house.

Nick and Stuart laughed again.

"Let's go, Waldo," said Marvin, tugging on the leash.

Waldo slowly got up, took a few more steps, then sat down again.

"He really knows how to walk a dog!" said Stuart. "No wonder Mrs. North chose him."

"And what would you do different?" asked Marvin.

"Did you hear something?" Stuart asked.

"No, I didn't hear anything," said Nick.

"I thought I heard someone talking to me," said Stuart. "It must have been the wind."

Instead of going around the block, Marvin only managed to go to the corner and back. At least he didn't have to use the pooper-scooper in front of Nick and Stuart. But Waldo hadn't eaten in two days. And if nothing goes in, nothing comes out.

He put Waldo back in the house.

"I'll be out in a second," he told his friends. "Then we can do something. Okay?"

He put the leash and pooper-scooper away.

Waldo lay on the floor, watching him with sad eyes.

"See you later, Waldo," said Marvin. *"Eat something."*

He checked to make sure he still had the key, then went outside, locking the door behind him.

Nick and Stuart were gone.

6

Some Dog Food Is Eaten

On Sunday, Waldo's bowl was still full of food.

Maybe the food had gone bad. It had been in his bowl since Wednesday night.

Marvin took the bowl into the garage and dumped it into Mrs. North's garbage can.

He returned to the kitchen. He found some green dish soap under the sink. He washed Waldo's bowl. Then he rinsed it a long time so it wouldn't taste like soap. He dried it with a dish towel, which he found in the drawer next to the sink.

Waldo watched him.

He filled the bowl with fresh dog food.

"Here you go," he said, setting it down in front of the old whisker-faced dog.

Waldo didn't even look at it.

Marvin picked out a piece of dog food and held it in front of Waldo's nose. "Yum, yum," he said.

Waldo turned his head away. He whined.

Marvin sat on the kitchen floor and stroked his back. "I tell you what," he said. "If I eat it, will you?"

The bit of dog food was still in his hand.

Marvin opened his mouth wide so Waldo could see. He took the bit of dog food between his thumb and forefinger and held it inside his mouth.

He was careful not to let it touch his tongue.

He quickly pulled out his hand, closed his mouth, and swallowed.

"Yum, delicious!" he said.

The dog food was hidden in his fist.

Waldo wasn't fooled.

"Okay," said Marvin. "I'll really eat it this time. But then you have to, too."

Waldo watched him.

Marvin touched the dog food with his tongue. It wasn't horrible. It tasted a little like cereal.

He bit into it.

It was chewier than cereal. And a little bit gritty, like it had tiny seeds in it.

He chewed and swallowed.

It wasn't gross. It wasn't something he'd ask his mom to get for an after-school snack. But it really wasn't too bad.

"Okay, your turn," he said.

Waldo whined.

"Like this," said Marvin. He crawled to Waldo's bowl and picked out a piece of

dog food with his teeth.

He chewed it up and swallowed. He smiled at Waldo. "Delicious!" he said.

Waldo lay his whiskered face against the floor.

7

Liver

"Have you tried liver?" asked Dr. Charles.

"Yes, my mom made it once. But I didn't like it," said Marvin.

"I mean, for Waldo," said the doctor.

"Oh."

It was Monday afternoon. Waldo still hadn't eaten, so Marvin called the vet on the telephone. Mrs. North had left the number.

Dr. Charles said that Waldo probably just missed Mrs. North.

He told Marvin what to do. Go to the

store and buy a quarter pound of liver. Boil it in water for ten minutes. Then cut it up in little pieces.

"And serve it to him on a real plate," Dr. Charles added. "Instead of his doggie bowl."

That made Marvin smile. "Okay," he said. "Thank you."

"Waldo's a funny dog," said Dr. Charles. "He's not sick. Just love-sick. Let me know what happens."

Marvin hung up the phone, feeling a little bit better.

He sat on the floor next to Waldo and petted him. "We'll both be glad when Mrs. North gets back," he said.

He'd had a rough day at school. "Miss Hillway treats me like I'm a criminal!" he told the love-sick dog.

Waldo pushed his head under Marvin's hand.

Marvin petted him. "Nick and Stuart hate me," he said. "They say I think I'm better than everyone. I don't think I'm better than everyone. I just have a job to do."

Waldo licked Marvin across the face with his big tongue.

Marvin petted him some more, then stood up. He checked to make sure the key was in his pocket. "I'll be back after dinner," he promised. *"With liver!"*

He tried his best to sound enthusiastic.

His mother said she'd take him to the store after dinner to buy the liver. And then drive him to Mrs. North's house.

"Can I come?" asked Jacob. "I've never seen the inside of a real teacher's house."

"Sure," said Marvin, glad to impress his older brother.

"Me too," said Linzy. "I want to meet Waldo."

Marvin's father went along too. "I don't want to be a party pooper," he said.

Marvin smiled. After all his troubles, it felt good to have his family with him.

He paid for the liver out of his own money. A quarter pound only cost 37¢. Less than a candy bar.

Inside Mrs. North's house, Marvin found a pot and filled it with water. He turned on the stove. His mother offered to cook the liver for him, but Marvin said, "No, it's part of my job."

He dropped the slimy meat into the boiling water.

Jacob was walking around the house. "Cool," he said as he went from one room to another.

Linzy hugged and petted and rolled around on the floor with Waldo. "I wuv you, Waldo," she said.

The liver was stinking up the kitchen.

Marvin let it boil for ten minutes, like Dr. Charles said. Then he plucked it out of the water with a fork and cut it up into bite-size pieces.

He really didn't think it would work. He had tasted liver. And he had tasted dog food.

He liked dog food better.

He put the liver on a regular plate and set it on the floor.

His family gathered around to watch.

"Look, Waldo, *liver!*" said Marvin.

Waldo didn't move.

"*Please,* Waldo," begged Linzy. She pushed the plate to him.

Waldo sniffed at it.

Then he stood up, stuck his head over the plate, and ate a piece of liver.

Marvin and his family cheered.

Waldo ate another piece, then another. He didn't stop until the plate was empty.

Then he waddled over to his dog food bowl and ate all his dog food too.

"All he needed was an appetizer," said Marvin's mother.

Marvin was so happy he almost cried.

He washed and dried the pot, knife, fork, and plate.

Linzy had to use the potty.

Of course! thought Marvin. She

couldn't go anywhere without needing to go to the bathroom. He smiled. He knew the kids in his class would be glad.

8
Where's Waldo?

Tuesday morning Marvin woke up with a start. He couldn't remember if he had locked Mrs. North's front door!

He remembered his family getting ready to leave. Then Linzy had to go to the bathroom. And Jacob was in a hurry because there was a TV show he wanted to watch. And Linzy had to hug Waldo three more times.

He got dressed quickly and rushed through breakfast.

He just couldn't remember.

As he rode his bike to Mrs. North's, he felt a knot in the pit of his stomach.

He dropped his bike in front of her house and ran to her front door.

He tried the knob.

It was locked.

But that didn't mean anything, he realized. The robbers could have locked it after they left.

He unlocked the door and stepped inside.

Everything seemed to be in order.

Except Waldo wasn't there to greet him.

"Waldo!" called Marvin. "Oh, Wal-do!"

The TV was still there. The VCR. There were no open drawers. Nothing seemed to be missing, except—

"Waldo!" Marvin called again.

He looked around the kitchen and the living room, then entered Mrs. North's bedroom. Something smelled funny.

Waldo had thrown up on the floor.

Marvin just missed stepping in it.

He could see pieces of liver and dog food. It looked like Waldo had thrown up everything he had eaten.

"Waldo!" Marvin called.

He looked under the bed.

Waldo lay there.

"There you are! You old whisker-faced dog!"

Waldo didn't move.

"Waldo!" he shouted. "Wake up, Waldo! Wake up, you stupid dog!"

But already he knew that Waldo would never wake up.

9

Do Something!

He didn't know what to do.

Waldo was dead. He threw up the liver and died.

Do something!

Should he call 911?

Do something! The words kept repeating inside his head. *Waldo is dead. Do something!*

Should he get him out from under the bed? How would he even do that? Pull him by the tail? And even if he could get him out from under the bed, then what?

He called home.

It rang eleven times. His parents had already left for work.

Do something!

"I never should have given him liver," he said.

He couldn't just leave Waldo there. Could he? Just go to school as if nothing happened?

He walked around the house. He looked at himself in the bathroom mirror and noticed for the first time that he was crying.

He wiped his eyes on his shirt sleeve.

He walked quickly back to the phone. He called the vet.

There was a recording. The office was closed until 10:00. But it gave another number to call in case of an emergency.

Marvin didn't know if it was an emergency. Waldo was already dead.

He dialed the emergency number anyway. Dr. Charles had said, "Let me know what happens."

A woman answered the phone. "Hello."

"Hello," said Marvin. "This is Marvin Redpost. I'm taking care of Mrs. North's dog, Waldo. I mean, I was. Dr. Charles said to let him know what happened. Well, he died. And I don't know what to do! I can't take him to a cemetery because—"

"I'll get my husband," said the woman. Dr. Charles came on the line.

"Waldo is under the bed," Marvin told him, trying not to cry. "He won't move. He threw up all his liver and dog food. I'm just here by myself."

"I'll be right over," said Dr. Charles. "Try to calm down. What's the address?"

Marvin thought a moment. "I don't

know," he said. "I know how to get here, but I don't know the address."

"Okay, then just tell me how to get there."

Marvin tried to think. "I don't know how to tell it," he said. He got an idea. "Wait, I'll go outside and check the street sign."

He set down the phone and started out the door.

Then he got a better idea. He had been bringing in Mrs. North's mail. He took an envelope back to the phone and read the address to Dr. Charles.

"You're doing just fine," said Dr. Charles. "I'll be there in fifteen minutes."

"He's in there. Under the bed," said Marvin, pointing to Mrs. North's bedroom.

He waited in another room until Dr. Charles was finished. He didn't look until after Waldo's body was inside Dr. Charles's van.

"Did the liver kill him?" Marvin asked. "Maybe I didn't cook it right?"

Dr. Charles smiled. "It wasn't because of anything you did, Marvin. Waldo was just a very old dog," he said. "His time had come."

Marvin watched the van drive away.

He cleaned up Waldo's throw-up and flushed it down the toilet. As Dr. Charles suggested, he poured a little vinegar over the spot to get rid of the smell.

He checked to make sure he still had the key, then locked the door behind him.

He rode his bike to school.

10
Ma

"Nice of you to show up, Marvin," said Miss Hillway as Marvin entered the classroom. He was twenty minutes late.

"Sorry," he said.

"Just waltz on in," said Miss Hillway. "We'll wait."

He quickly took his seat.

Miss Hillway handed out a worksheet.

Marvin started to write his name at the top. He wrote: *Ma*. That was as far as he got.

He tried not to think about Waldo—
the way he always wanted to be petted, his
white whiskers, his whining that sounded
like singing.

He took a deep breath.

And what about Mrs. North? What was she going to do when she came home? *Tomorrow night!*

Marvin imagined her opening her front door. She'd be surprised because Waldo wasn't there to greet her.

In his mind, Marvin saw her going through the house with her suitcase still in her hand. She was calling, "Waldo? Waldo? Wa-wa-wa-Waldo?" And then he saw her picking up the telephone.

He imagined himself alone in his room as the phone downstairs was ringing.

Miss Hillway came around and collected the worksheets.

"Ma?" she said, looking at Marvin's paper.

"Um, may I have more time?" he asked.

"I want Mrs. North to see this," said Miss Hillway, snapping up his paper.

At recess, Marvin walked off by himself.

Judy Jasper and Casey Happleton came running up to him.

"Hey, Marvin!" said Judy, out of breath. "What are you eating under there?"

"What?" he said.

"What are you eating under there?" asked Casey.

He didn't know what they were talking about. "Under where?" he asked.

The two girls roared with laughter. "You're eating your underwear!" exclaimed Judy.

"You said you were eating your under-wear," Casey explained.

"Leave me alone," said Marvin, walking away.

"It's just a joke!" said Casey. "What a crab!"

"Oh, there's Justin," said Judy. "Hey, Justin! What are you eating under there?"

"Under where?" asked Justin.

After school, it felt strange not to have to go to Mrs. North's house. Marvin felt empty.

"Are you okay?" Patsy Gatsby asked him.

He shrugged.

"Oh, he thinks he's better than everyone," said Stuart, coming up behind them. Nick was with Stuart.

"Shut up!" said Marvin.

"I don't have to!" said Nick.

Marvin glared at Nick. "Waldo's dead," he said. "Are you happy now?"

Nick's mouth dropped open.

"What happened?" asked Patsy.

Marvin told them how Waldo wouldn't eat. And about the liver. And then what he found this morning.

"Promise you won't tell anyone, okay?" he asked.

They promised.

"Oh, man," said Nick. "You are the unluckiest kid in the whole world."

11
Waiting

The worst part was waiting. Just waiting.

"Will you take me to see Waldo?" Linzy asked during dinner.

He hadn't told his family yet.

"I *wuv* Waldo," said Linzy.

"I don't think it's a good idea," said Marvin.

"Why not?" Linzy demanded.

"It just isn't," said Marvin.

"Can I go with Marvin to see Waldo?" Linzy asked her mother.

"It's not up to me," said Mrs. Redpost. "It's up to Marvin." She looked at Marvin.

"And I know you always consider your sister's feelings, don't you, Marvin?"

"Please, Marvin!" said Linzy. "I'll let you come to my birthday party."

Marvin sighed. "Sorry," he said. He tried to think of a nice way to put it. "Waldo's not there anymore."

"Where'd he go?" asked Linzy.

"He's in heaven, with the angels."

"Oh no!" said Mrs. Redpost, dropping her fork.

"Oh, you mean he's dead," said Linzy. She crunched into her pickle.

She didn't cry until an hour and a half later. When she went to bed. Right after she said a prayer "for Waldo in heaven."

Marvin's parents tried to make him feel better.

"It wasn't your fault," said his mother. "You know that."

"Do you want me to talk to Mrs. North for you?" asked his father.

"No," said Marvin.

When he got to school Wednesday morning, he was mobbed by the kids in his class.

"Did you kill Mrs. North's dog?" asked Justin.

"He forgot to feed him," said Melanie. "The poor dog starved to death."

"I heard he choked to death," said Kenny. "On a piece of liver."

Marvin looked around. He knew Stuart and Patsy could keep a secret. It must have been Nick.

"What do you think Mrs. North is going to do?" asked Casey.

"She'll flunk you for sure," said Justin.

"If you're lucky," said Warren.

"I'd move to another state if I were you," said Gina.

"I'd move to another country," said Heather.

"You can go to jail for murdering someone's dog," said Judy.

Clarence and Travis joined the group.

"Hey, Marvin?" asked Travis. "Did you shoot Mrs. North's dog?"

"Got him right in the liver!" said Clarence.

The rest of the day was just a blur to Marvin. He couldn't pay attention. He just kept thinking one thought. *Mrs. North will be home tonight!*

Miss Hillway said good-bye to the class. "Thank you. It was a most enjoyable week. You've been a wonderful class." She looked at Marvin. "Of course, there are always a *few exceptions.* Mrs. North will get a full report."

"Do you want to come over to my house?" Stuart asked as they walked out of class together.

"No," said Marvin.

Now that Waldo was dead, Marvin's friends liked him again.

"Why not?" asked Nick. "It's not like you have to go to Mrs. North's!"

"I just want to be alone," said Marvin.

"Did the vet tell you what time Waldo died?" asked Stuart.

"No," said Marvin.

"You should ask him," said Stuart. "They can figure those things out. Because if Waldo died before midnight, then Mrs. North only has to pay you for five days. Fifteen dollars. But if he died after midnight, then she has to pay you for six days. Eighteen dollars."

Stuart was good at math.

"I guess you don't get the four-dollar bonus," said Nick.

Marvin walked home. Then he got on his bike and rode to Mrs. North's house for the last time. He still had to bring in her newspaper and mail.

Her house felt empty, like a cave.

He wrote her a note.

> Dear Mrs. North,
>
> If you are looking around for Waldo, don't. You won't find him. He's not in your house. And he's not outside. Well, he's dead. I hope you had a nice time on your trip.
>
> Yours truly,
> Marvin Redpost

He went home and waited for Mrs. North to call.

"Do you think I'll be expelled?" he asked Jacob.

"I don't think she can do that," said Jacob. "It's not like you did it on purpose."

"I just did what the doctor told me," said Marvin.

"But she'll still blame you," said Jacob. "She might say she doesn't. But really she will. Every time she looks at you. Every time she gives you a grade. She'll be thinking, 'Marvin Redpost. He's the boy who killed my dog.'"

Jacob patted Marvin on the back. "You'd be better off if you were expelled," he said.

The phone rang.

Marvin felt his heart jump.

But it was just one of his mother's friends.

He went to bed at nine o'clock and lay awake for at least two hours.

Mrs. North never called.

12

I'm Sorry

Marvin tapped the red post—for luck—then bravely walked to school.

He entered his classroom.

Mrs. North wasn't there.

"Have you talked to Mrs. North yet?" asked Casey. "What are you going to say to her?"

Marvin shrugged.

"Man, I can't believe you're here," said Clarence. "If I were you, I'd be in Mexico."

No one got close to him, not even Nick or Stuart. No one wanted to be seen with him when Mrs. North walked in.

The bell rang.

Marvin kept his eyes on the door.

"She probably can't stop crying," said Melanie. "That's why she's not here."

Maybe she never came home, thought Marvin. That's why she never called. Maybe she had such a good time on her trip, she decided to stay *forever!* Maybe she fell in love with someone. And she's sailing around the world with him.

Mrs. North walked through the door. "Good morning, everyone," she said. "It's nice to see you again."

She glanced at Marvin, then turned her head away.

He looked down at his desk. He thought he saw a flash of hatred in her eyes.

"Well, let's see if anyone learned anything while I was gone," she said. "This won't be graded. I just want to see how far you got. Gina."

Mrs. North handed a stack of tests to Gina, and Gina passed them out.

Marvin set right to work. He didn't dare take his eyes off the paper.

Mrs. North was walking around the room. Marvin wasn't looking, but somehow he knew.

She was coming toward him. He could feel it in his bones.

The room got very quiet.

She was getting closer.

He tried to focus on his work.

She was right beside him. He could see her shoes.

He closed his eyes. Her cold hand touched the back of his neck.

"Come on, Marvin, we need to talk."

He stood up. Every eye in the classroom watched as Mrs. North led him outside. There was dead silence.

"I'm sorry," said Mrs. North.

"*You're* sorry?" said Marvin. His legs were shaking.

"It was unfair of me to ask you to take care of such an old—" She stopped. "I just didn't want to put him in a kennel. You must have felt awful!"

The next thing Marvin knew, Mrs. North was hugging him.

"The plane was very late," she said, still hugging him. "Otherwise I would have called you last night. You probably thought I hated you."

"Maybe a little," said Marvin.

She let go of him. "I spoke to Dr. Charles this morning," she said. "He told me what you did. I'm so glad Waldo had someone like you."

Marvin noticed her eyes were wet.

"Liver was his favorite," said Mrs. North. "He died happy."

She paid him the money she owed him. She gave him twenty-five dollars, as promised.

"I'd like to do something special for you, too," she said. "How about I take you out to lunch this weekend? You pick the restaurant."

"Okay," said Marvin.

She hugged him again. "He had a good life," she said.

They walked back into the classroom.

Everyone was watching. And wondering.

Marvin kept his head down. *Let them wonder,* he thought.

He sat at his desk and returned to his test.

Casey Happleton stared at him. Her ponytail stuck out of the side of her head. Her finger was in her mouth.

"Wait, let me get this straight," Nick said at recess. "She's taking you out to lunch *because* her dog died."

"Twenty-five dollars!" said Stuart.

"And he only had to take care of the dog for five days instead of seven."

"What restaurant are you going to choose?" asked Nick.

Marvin shrugged.

"Man, you're so lucky," said Nick. "It's unfair. Some people have all the luck."

"Mr. and Mrs. Redpost," he said. "I have something important to tell you."

"Mr. and Mrs. Redpost?" asked Mrs. Redpost.

He took a breath. He wasn't quite sure how to say it.

"Marvin Redpost is dead," said Marvin.

From *Marvin Redpost: Kidnapped at Birth?* by Louis Sachar

Marvin felt terrible. In fifty years they'll dig up the time capsule. And they'll find out a boy named Marvin Redpost picked his nose. And everyone will laugh at him.

Maybe in fifty years he'd be president! But then they'd dig up the time capsule and say, "You can't be president anymore. You picked your nose."

It wasn't fair.

From *Marvin Redpost: Why Pick on Me?* by Louis Sachar

Marvin waved the bat back and forth.

He was afraid of Clarence but tried not to show it.

Suddenly Clarence laughed.

Then everyone else laughed too.

The umpire spoke to Marvin. "I'm sorry, young man," he said. "But you can't play. You're out of uniform."

"Huh?" asked Marvin.

He looked down at his clothes. He was wearing a dress.

From *Marvin Redpost: Is He a Girl?* by Louis Sachar

About the Author

In order to research this book, Louis Sachar actually tasted dog food. "It's just the way I described it in the book," says Louis. "Like cereal. But kind of gritty."

Louis Sachar lives in Austin, Texas, with his wife, Carla, their daughter, Sherre, and the family dog, Lucky (who loves liver). He modeled Waldo after his next-door neighbor's dog, Cartouche.